Grosvenor House
Publishing Limited

This book is published by
Grosvenor House Publishing Ltd
Link House
140 The Broadway, Tolworth, Surrey, KT6 7HT.
www.grosvenorhousepublishing.co.uk

A CIP record for this book
is available from the British Library

ISBN 978-1-80381-461-2

Acknowledgements

A huge thanks to the wonderful team of people
that have helped me to bring this book to publication.
To my editor and friend Cate Palmer who has helped
me to shape this beautiful story, whilst always making
me cry with laughter until my tummy hurts.

Thank you, as always, to the long suffering Julie
at Grosvenor House for her support,
guidance and massive amounts of patience.

To my family and friends, thank you for listening to me
and encouraging me to never give up on my dreams.

And to everyone that loves owls as
much as I do...this one's for you.

There once was an owl that lived in the woods

High up in an old oak tree.

He had a brother called Merlin, a sister called Eve,

Clarence loved all his owl family.

But one day poor Clarence woke up and he found

That his hoot, it was no longer there,

And although he still looked like a white fluffy owl,

He sounded just like a brown bear.

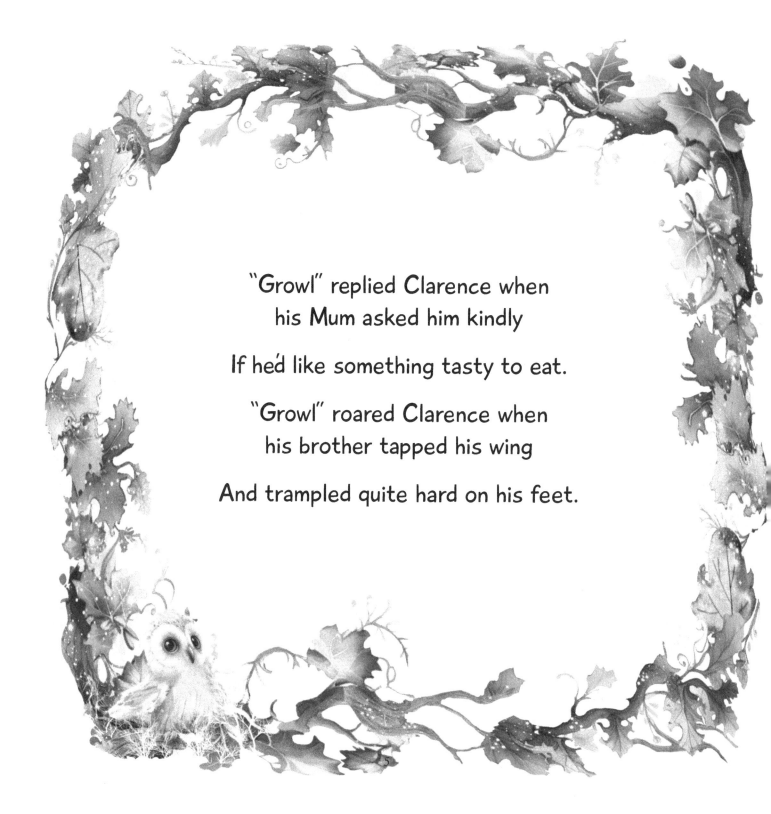

"Growl" replied Clarence when
his Mum asked him kindly

If he'd like something tasty to eat.

"Growl" roared Clarence when
his brother tapped his wing

And trampled quite hard on his feet.

Clarence felt grumpy, he didn't know why,

He felt quite confused and quite sad.

He wanted to tuck his head under his wing

And stop making a noise that was bad.

His father sat with him on a cold snowy branch

"Dear Clarence please tell me what's wrong,

No one feels happy all of the time

But I'm here to help you feel strong".

"Let out your growl, as loud as you can

Don't keep it all bottled inside.

Don't be afraid to say how you feel,

I will always be here by your side".

Clarence gave out a big growl, then a sigh,

A big tear rolled right down his cheek,

But just sitting here with wise Daddy owl

Had made him feel able to speak.

It felt good to be able to talk to someone

And let out his big angry growl.

He felt better and more like his old happy self

Instead of a grumpy young owl.

16

Clarence ruffled his feathers and puffed out his chest

He knew just what he had to do,

And instead of a roar, or a squeak or a growl

He let out a huge twit twooooooo.

"Hurray" hooted Clarence, "Hoot hoot hoot, hurray".

He smiled at his wise Daddy owl,

"I feel so much better, now that I know

That sometimes it's ok to growl".

Clarence flew over to Merlin and Eve,

"I'm feeling much better" he said,

"I know it's important to say how I feel

Rather than keeping it all in my head".

His family all hugged their dear little owl

Up high in the old oak tree.

And they hooted together through
the cold winter's night,

One big happy owl family.

About the Author

Elizabeth Green was born and raised in Bolton, Lancashire but now resides in North Yorkshire with her husband, two dogs and two cats. Elizabeth LOVES owls and is dedicated to supporting local sanctuaries and helping to preserve our owl population.

Elizabeth is the author of the "Detective Dopeyworth" series.

Find Elizabeth on Instagram @author_elizabethgreen and Facebook @ElizabethGreensAuthorPage

Praise for Elizabeth's books.

"Full of humour and fun, we loved this book. It is perfect for young readers".

"When is the next one coming out? I loved it".

"A lovely, uplifting and amusing book".

"Elizabeth has such a beautiful writing style and writes from the heart".

Milton Keynes UK
Ingram Content Group UK Ltd.
UKHW050828231023
431156UK00008B/56

A Rat for Mouse

written by Jenny Alexander
illustrated by Steve Smallman

Everyone loved Mouse and
Jojo's new hamster, Jumbo.
They thought he was sweet
and funny. But Mouse was
not very keen on him.
"He is too shy, and he hides
all the time," he said.
"You should like him, then,"
said Jojo. "He's just like you!"

Mouse wanted another pet.
"There are two of us, so
we should have two pets,"
he said.
Jojo liked the idea of having
Jumbo all to herself. They
went to ask their mum.

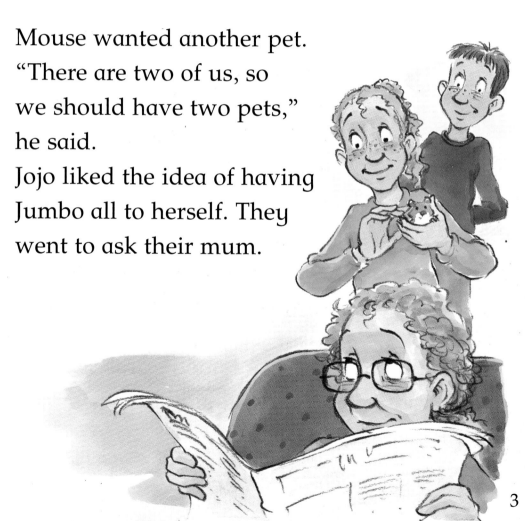

3

The next day, Mr Macdonald took Mouse to the pet shop. He thought Mouse would choose another rabbit.

But Mouse did not want another rabbit. He could never love another rabbit as much as he had loved Lucky.

They looked at fish

and birds.

They looked at gerbils,

guinea pigs

and chinchillas.

Nothing seemed quite right.

But then Mouse saw the rat. He was
in a cage on his own, eating a sunflower
seed. His front paws were like tiny pink
hands. He stopped eating, and looked
at Mouse.

"This is what I want!" cried Mouse.

"But Mouse," said his dad. "That is a rat."

The shopkeeper said that rats made very good pets. They were clean and clever. But they were not like other animals. A rat was a one-person pet. He would love his owner and never hurt him, but he would probably not let other people pick him up.

The shopkeeper told Mouse, "You should only choose a rat if you are sure you can love him and look after him, because he will not let anyone else do it for you."

"I am sure," said Mouse.

Mouse wanted to stroke the rat,
but the man said he would have
to get the rat's trust first.
It would take several days.

"Just put your hand inside the cage
and let him sniff it," he said. "Don't try
to handle him until he comes to you,
or he might bite you."

They chose a cage with a

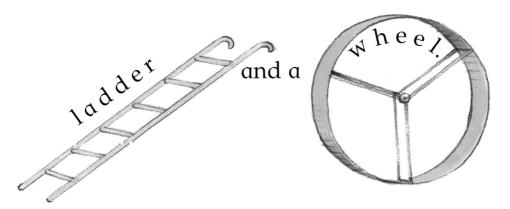

ladder and a wheel.

Mouse was very excited. He could not wait to get home and show the others his new pet.

But when his mum saw it, her mouth fell open.

That is a rat!

THIS RAT MIGHT BITE!

Mouse explained that rats made
very good pets. Jojo wanted to pick
the rat up, but Mouse said,
"You can't. He won't let you."
He told them what the
pet shop man had said.
Then he made a sign
and stuck it on the cage.

It said, "This rat might bite."

Mouse called his rat Ricky. Every day, when he fed Ricky, he put his hand inside the cage, and let the rat sniff him.

He had to be very brave,
because sometimes Ricky
opened his mouth and
put his teeth round
Mouse's finger. His
teeth were long and yellow.
But he never bit Mouse.

On the third day,
Ricky walked onto
Mouse's hand.

He ran up Mouse's arm,

and darted inside
his sweatshirt.

He ran up and down
inside his sleeve.

After that, Mouse's rat
went everywhere with him.
He shared Mouse's meals.

He helped Mouse
with his homework.

He curled up in his
cage at night, right next
to Mouse's bed.

But Ricky was not sure about anyone else.
He would let people stroke him, but
he would never let them pick him up.

One day, when the friends were watching television, Ricky took Ben's biscuit. Without thinking, Ben made a grab for him.

The rat spun round and sank his teeth into Ben's finger.

Ben let out a yell,

and Mrs Macdonald
came rushing in.

Ricky let go and
ran back to Mouse.

21

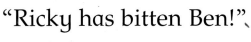
"Ricky has bitten Ben!"
cried Jojo.
"You will have to
take him back to the
pet shop," said Sam.

Mrs Macdonald
made Ben put his
finger under the
cold tap.
"Perhaps a rat isn't
a good pet after all,"
she said.

Mouse was angry.
"It was not Ricky's fault!"
he protested. "You all
know what the man from
the pet shop said. Ben
should not have grabbed
him like that."

Ben agreed.
"Mouse is right.
I should not have
tried to pick Ricky
up. I just forgot."

After that, no one forgot again. Everyone was a bit scared of Mouse's rat. They thought he was fierce and dangerous.

But Mouse **adored** him.